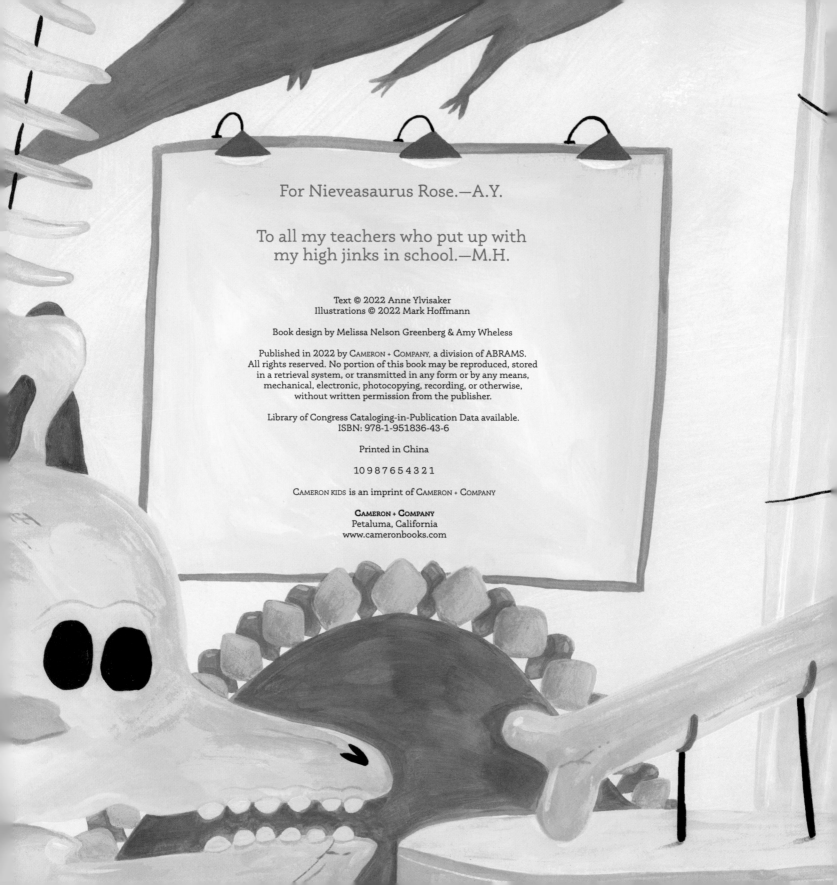

For Nieveasaurus Rose.—A.Y.

To all my teachers who put up with
my high jinks in school.—M.H.

Text © 2022 Anne Ylvisaker
Illustrations © 2022 Mark Hoffmann

Book design by Melissa Nelson Greenberg & Amy Wheless

Library of Congress Cataloging-in-Publication Data available.
ISBN: 978-1-951836-43-6

Printed in China

10 9 8 7 6 5 4 3 2 1

CAMERON KIDS is an imprint of CAMERON + COMPANY

CAMERON + COMPANY
Petaluma, California
www.cameronbooks.com

IAMASAURUS

ANNE YLVISAKER AND MARK HOFFMANN

cameron kids

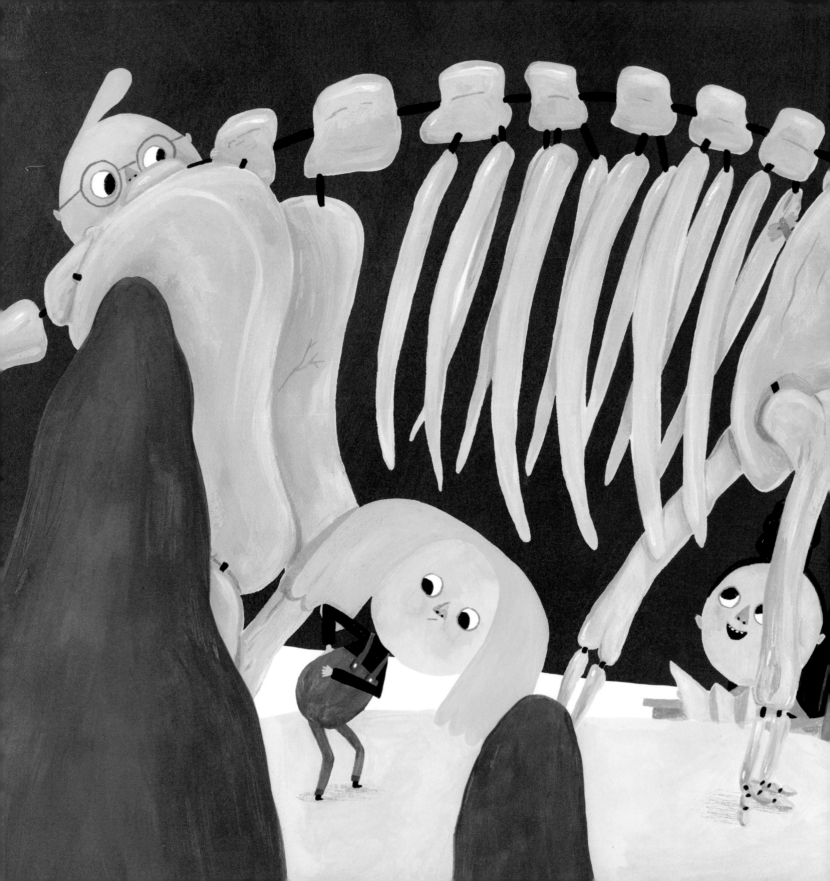

Iamasaurus!

I am Noodlevorous,
one of the genus *Ridiculorous.*

Mothers abhor us.
Babies adore us.
We romp and we stomp and
we chomp on the floras.

WE'VE GOT

MAXILLAE

MANDIBLES

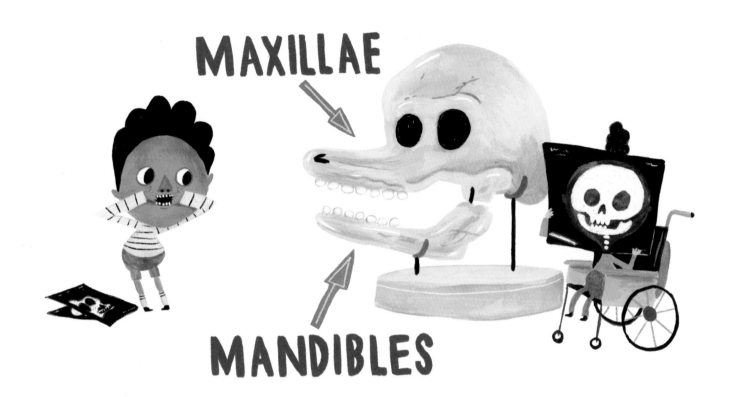

CLAVICLES

RIBS

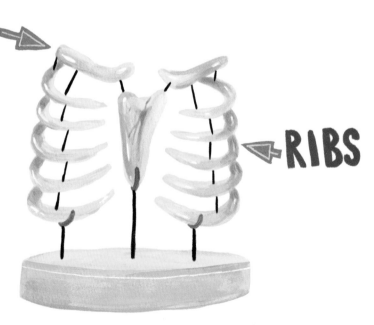

We're explorers,
outdoorers.
We travel in herds.
Don't try to catch us,
we'll fly off like birds.

ABDOMINIS

SOLEI

LATISSIMUS DORSI

We're stronger than elephants,
faster than bats.

Our footprints strike terror
in uncles and aunts.

WE'VE GOT

RETINAS

CORNEAS

LENSES

IRISES

We see you,
we hear you,
but we don't understand.
Our language consists of
grunts and demands.

We're performers,
transformers.
We hang upside down.
If you don't feed us soon,
we'll devour the town.

You can join us;
you've got your own
loud vocal cords.

We're a chorus.
Let's ROARus!

MAY   2022